CW00859736

Jasmine Emelie

Pls,
MAKE ME SCREAM
LESBIAN Short Story

Pls, Make Me Scream.

(A part of "We should all be fucking" Anthology)

Jasmine Emelie

Table of Contents

Copyright

Copyright@2022 Jasmine Emelie

All rights reserved

No parts of this book may be reproduced in any form or by any electronic or mechanical means including information storage or retrieval systems, without written permission from the author, except in the case of usage in a book review.

Disclaimer

The characters in this book are entirely fictional, any resemblance to an actual person, living or dead, is entirely coincidental

Dedication

To the wild ones, the screamers and those that love the pain.

Under the warmth of her skin, my body is trapped in between her and the bed, sweat dripping down the sheets as she takes my lips in hers and devours them in her hungry mouth.

She tastes likes strawberries and what the ocean might taste of when the sun sets in it. So I dive deeper, drowning on her lips with each kiss, my tongue gliding against hers as I moan into her in quiet melodies of pleasure – body trembling underneath her lean frame with my arms wrapped around her neck – fingers combing into her dark curly hair.

Tola was so many things. She was my friend and neighbor, but above all... she was a beast.

She wanted it how she wanted it, and my body was always ready to please her in every way that it could. It bled in several colors of pain and pleasure, and I screamed along with it – every single time she drew those emotions out of me.

"Mi Amor," she whispers on my lips, her hand tight against the back of my neck – nails cutting into my skin. The pain starts as a mellow sting, then digs its way into my core as it bursts into sharp prickles that run down to my clit and tug at it.

Tola kisses me harder, pressing her plump lips against mine and sucking the air out of me. But I want to hear more of it; I want to hear her say the words, again and again, to call me that which tells the world that I am hers and hers alone.

"Mi Amor." Her voice wavers as the soft curves of her hips grind against mine, one hand wrapped around my petite breast, squeezing the soft flesh in hard grips and sending shock waves of pain through me. "I want to feel inside you."

My clit twitches, dancing in mad pulses as she rubs against it, the feel of her wetness slicing through mine as she thrusts herself back and forth, like a swing swaying softly in the breeze.

I want to have all of her; I want to be consumed by her heat and scorching desire – my hips meeting hers, twisting and turning as much as she would let me; my body trembling on the sheets in slight quivers and mellow vibrations as I die slowly from her sweet torture.

Each second stretches into a timeline; each breath I take escapes as a soft gasp, tumbling off my lips and slipping into hers.

Tola was going to be the death of me. I dip in and out of myself, my eyes fluttering shut and swinging wide open as she grinds harder into me and tightens her fingers some more, around my throat.

It was hard to breathe. Air flowed in and out of me, in quick and shallow puffs, as my body quivered and my clit throbbed. I thrust my chest forward, my breast getting lost under hers – squashed underneath their firm weight, with her nipples hard against my chest.

She is a drug – my drug – and I wanted more of her, more of the pain she inflicts in slow strides, more of her rough kisses and her firm grips. I wanted to feel every part of her on me. In me. Everywhere.

I bet she knew just that: how much I craved her and needed her touch, cause I knew she needed to touch me just as much.

"I want to make you scream," Tola whispers on my lips, her breath hot against my skin. It feels like hundreds of tiny jolts of electricity racing down my body in slow strides – right from my lips, down to my toes.

Then those lips of hers trail down to my neck. She kisses so softly, pressing briefly against my skin for the smallest of seconds before she pulls away and travels lower – down to my shoulders. The torture continues once more, with the slightest touch of her lips on my skin, right before she buries her teeth in my shoulder.

I'm dripping. My pussy pulsates in wild pumps, twitching and tugging ceaselessly, and I tremble along with it – my eyes closed tight as I die under her soft kisses and painful bites.

"I want to hear you beg." She sits up and my eyes flutter open.

Tola's gaze pierces deep into mine. Promises as endless as the stars swim through the dark pools of her brown eyes as her fingers dance against the slippery surface of my skin. They leave goosebumps in their path, long nails drawing constellations of nameless shapes and patterns, and my body shivers underneath. "Would you like that, Dara…?"

But I can't answer. The words form in my throat and melt into quiet, breathy moans just before they leave my lips, so I do nothing but stare as her gaze falls from my face and comes down on my tits.

Her chest heaves in quiet beats as she stares at my tits, breast round and full, rising and falling on her – her nipples the color of chocolate, hard and erect on her areola. I wanted to taste her.

"You are so beautiful, Mi Amor."

She leans down and takes my breast in her mouth, sucking and nibbling on each of them; biting and licking on my nipples as she swipes her tongue over the hard knob in slow circles that leave me shuddering on the bed.

"And you taste so good." She says the words with my breast full in her mouth, glancing up at me as her hand skims down the sides of my stomach, her fingernails dragging against my skin in slow, deep scratches.

A shiver runs through me as her hand wedges itself between our thighs – crawling past our sweat-soaked skin till it brushes against the soft curls of my bush.

"Gaaaawd!" I scream as she shoves her fingers inside me – my head slamming back into the bed as my eyes drift shut.

I shudder all over as three long digits slide in and out with fervent thrusts that dare to tear me apart. They twist and turn in scattered directions and into narrow spaces; they dig and shove into me till I'm nothing but a ball of nerves, all lit up and burning with ecstasy.

It's always a wonder what Tola could do with her fingers. They move in and out of me like silent killers, their thick build stretching my insides apart with every jab, sliding through my tight passage with its tip crooked upwards and fingernails grazing along my insides.

It's euphoric. It's torture. And I want more.

A soft chuckle slips out of Tola's lips as her teeth clamp down on my nipple, her eyes fluttering open – staring right at me – as she chews down on it with a cruel bite.

I howl in decibels and octaves, my back arched as I thrust my breast further into her. And Tola rewards me with more pain, fitting my entire tits in her mouth and piercing her fangs into the soft flesh of my breast.

"You like it when it hurts, Mi Amor?" She asks as her mouth draws back from my breast and her tongue takes over. It swirls over my areola, rubs around my nipples in small circles, then its tip, wags furiously on them, right before she takes the hard knobs in her mouth and sucks on them with hard suctions – one at a time.

Waves of ecstasy, rise and crash into me in high tides. They leave me breathless and hot all over, my body vibrating as I run my fingers through her tight curls, wrap them around my fingers and yank hard at them.

A low growl rings in Tola's throat. She pulls three fingers out of me and slides four back in, digging into me like a mad beast, "Scream for me, Mi Amor."

The sounds spill out of my lips as she starts fucking me with mad thrusts, shoving her fingers so deep down to my cervix, with my nipples searing in her hot mouth, as she sucks on them with long, hard pulls.

"Oh Gaaawd, yes… deeper. Take it deeper!" The words tumble out of my lips in shrill tones as my body trembles and vibrate.

But Tola doesn't head to my plea. She stops thrusting her fingers and starts wagging them. They slide left and right in quick movements, pulling my insides with them as my body shakes in wild tremors – my eyes shut tight.

I moan in mantras and solicitations to gods that I don't know; I cry out Tola's name and she rewards me, placing her thumb on my clit and rubbing it in wild circles – the hard button strumming in sweet pleasures of pain. And I die all over again.

I cum with a piercing shriek, my legs going numb as they clamp tight around her hand – my clit pulsating wildly underneath her torturous thumb as I shudder and tremble from the sweet sensation. The sweet, tingly feeling course all over me in slow strides, then pick up the pace and run through me – every part of me – down to my toes, till my entire being engulfs in it.

It feels like the earth shattered and I fell into it; falling into a pool of pleasure that supersedes any I'd ever hard. The feeling is so strong – so powerful – that I lose breath and go weak.

"Oh, Mi Amor," Tola sits up and glances down at me with a smile on her lips. She pulls her fingers out of me and takes them in her mouth, sucking my juices off them, one finger at a time. "You taste so good."

Tola's eyes are closed tight like she's praying to a deity. Her breathing turns quick and shallow, her breasts swaying in quiet swings.

There has always been something so mesmerizing about her breasts. They spill out of her chest in large oval pairs, her dark areola a beautiful contrast to her brown skin – nipples hard and erect. She's breath-taking.

I grab onto her tits, hands trembling slightly, and squeeze hard. Tola's soft flesh pops through the spaces in between each finger. She moans in soft groans, throwing her head backward, her dark curls swaying behind her.

Her breasts are so soft, the large globes sinking in at my slightest touch – just like jelly. I roll each nipple between a thumb and a forefinger and watch Tola shudder. It's a rare sight – to see her so vulnerable, and I wanted nothing more than to capture that moment and have it saved forever.

"Mi Amor," she gasps as I pinch on her nipples, twisting the hard thing in my fingers. But not for long.

Tola pushes my hands off her and covers my breast with hers. Her fingers dance around my nipples, grazing slightly on them before she grips my tits in a firm grasp, and kneads them like a chunk of dough.

"Let me take care of you, Mi Amor," she leans down and takes my nipples in her mouth again, nibbling briefly on them, then her lips travel lower, down my stomach –

dropping feathery kisses on me, till she got to my thighs, "let me eat you."

Tola pulls my thighs apart, her hands hot against my skin, and buries her head in between my legs; she grabs my ass, her nails digging into my soft flesh and her tongue sliding deep inside me.

"Yeeees!" I cry out, shutting my eyes tight as tears slide down the sides of my temples.

No one but her could do that, could please me and tear me apart at the same time. No matter what she does, or how she does it, it leaves me sizzling with pleasure – my entire body coursing with the euphoric sensation that I have only ever read in books.

It was bliss.

Tola shoves her stiff tongue in and out of me with mad thrusts, a quiet moan on her lips as she eats me out without a break.

Her fingers run up from my ass to my hips as she grips tight on my waist. Then she pulls her tongue out of me and drags it across my slit, a shiver running down my spine as she slips it through my slit and presses it hard against my clit.

Tola tongues the hard knob till I'm thrashing on the bed, my legs vibrating as I thrust my hips in her face – my hands in her hair, pulling her deeper into me.

I gasped and moaned in shrill notes, my body trembling as my orgasm shoots through me. It pours out in a wild rush and drowns Tola in a sea of warm saltiness.

Tomorrow will be my turn; tomorrow I'll make her scream.

Pls, Eat Me Out

There was jazz playing somewhere in the back, the sweet melody caressing my fears into submission, drowning me in their blues – in deep percussions and mellow strings. I held my hands in a tight grip – crisscrossed fingers placed on my thighs, the pair trembling in quiet vibrations.

"You good Ara?" Deze asked, placing her hand on my bare thigh and squeezing tight – soft tingles racing down my spine.

"Um… yeah… good, I'm good." The words leave my mouth in hurried breaths; in trembling tones and wavering syllables.

"That's nice to hear." A smile breaks on Deze's small face, her lips dragging up her cheeks and exposing a dazzling set of whites.

Then her hand leaves my thigh, sliding off in a slow fall – her fingertips lingering for long seconds that seemed to stretch into hours.

I hold my breath, my eyes straining to look at hers unwavering, but I fail miserably, blinking rapidly as the last of her finger glides off my skin.

For the longest time I'd known Deze she almost, always, has a smile perched on her heart-shaped face. It would beam from a distance as far as a mile, her gap tooth clear as day. But at that moment, her face contours into what must have been her neutral look, but to me, it was such an oddity.

"But you know, you don't have to do this," she said, her voice a low whisper, "we can call it quits if you want."

Her dreads, long with tips dipped in the brightest of maroon, swing from her face and brush against the base of her freckled neck. I wanted to run my hands through them, feel their softness, wrap them around my fingers and yank them till her scalp burned with searing pain.

"No," I squeaked, "I'm good."

Then Oma walked in, her wide hips swaying left and right. I followed their every movement – every dip and curve, every ripple and thrust. Oma was gorgeous, bathed in the color of the darkest nights with her white hair highlighting her melanin skin – hair cut so short it stood just inches from her scalp in smooth waves that seemed to never end.

"Hey." She spoke. Her voice was deep and smooth, the sound lingering in my consciousness as I stared with my mouth wide open. Time seemed to stand still, the air losing its oxygen as my gaze descends to her chest – her breast small and pointy, with nipples protruding through the thin fabric of her shirt.

"Hi," I responded, but my voice trembles and my clit follow suit. It quakes and shudders, sending slight tingles to my pulsating sex as it swells and engorges.

"I'm really happy you agreed to do this." Oma took a seat right beside me on the bed, her smooth skin rubbing against my bare thigh as her fingers climbed up the curves of my waist, leaving goosebumps along the way. "I've wanted to fuck you for a very long time."

I tried not to move, not to make a sound; my breathing, slow and shallow as my body shudders from her long, slender fingers – but quiet moans find their way out my lips.

Oma was a quiet one, barely making a sound, but her breathing became rasp as she drags her hands over my stomach and up to my chest, cupping my breast through the light cotton of my gown. She wasn't what I expected. Her grip is the softest touch, fondling my breast with little pulls and gentle squeezes.

"No bra, huh?" she dips her head and buries it in the crook of my neck, nuzzling on my skin – a quiet groan bustling from her throat, "Oma likes."

A fluttering storm rages in my stomach and crashes into my aching pussy. It throbs and twitches, my juices dripping out my slit in thick, creamy strands. I wanted to say something – to do something — but all I did was vibrate under her gentle touches, moaning in breathy gasps and quiet screams as she played with my tits.

But that was just the beginning.

Wet lips brush against my skin, they press hard into my neck and my breath catches in my throat. Oma kisses along the curves of my neck, lips like hot coal burns into me as they travel up my slender throat, up to my earlobes, then clamp down and suck on it.

"Do want me to take it slow…" she squeezes hard on my breast, turning and twisting in painful grips, "…or would you like it a little rough?"

I moan through clenched teeth, eyes drifting shut as I tremble on the bed. A mellow heat burns through my skin and disperses to every inch of me in smoldering waves, legs spreading wide open on their own accord as Oma nibbles on my ear with slow pulls – then sinks her teeth into the soft skin.

"I can bet she's a screamer," Deze said, her eyes fixed on my kneaded breast as she hooked her fingers in the straps of her gown and pulled it down, "and I want to be one to make her scream."

Large breast spills out of her gown in wild jiggles, her dark nipples standing erect on wide areolas.

I try to keep my eyes open, to focus on Deze as she takes slow steps towards me – her breast swaying like leaves caught in a gentle evening breeze – but my eyes drift shut as Oma's mouth leaves my earlobes and drags itself along the lines of my jaw, up my chin and then over my lips.

Her lips move roughly over mine, like the dance of raging spirits, biting and sucking with hard draws that leave me numb and aching for more. I can taste her. I can taste the hibiscus and ginger from her hungry mouth, a mixture of spicy and sweet that overpowers my senses and draws a howling moan out of me as she twists and squeezes my nipples in a tight grip.

Oma swallows it. She swallows my moans and screams as she deepens the kiss – her hands merciless on my breasts as they press and knead and mold them into objects unknown.

Then I felt it, warm hands clasping down on my thighs and spreading them further apart. A sharp sting shoots through me as Deze drags them wider. I force my eyes open and stare down at her, a breathy gasp leaving my lips as Oma grabs hold of my nipples again and twists them between her powerful fingers.

"You are so freaking wet." Deze leans forward, her head bent low as she plants it in between my legs, just inches away from my throbbing pussy lips, "You've wanted this for a long time, haven't you?"

***

If you enjoyed this snippet, click here to read the entire story.

To The Girls From Last Night

Dear you,

Yes, you both, the girls that took me from the bar last night and spread me open on the wild fields behind the church.

Bola and Kamsi.

You never said much cause your lips were occupied; one on my breast as you sucked and nibbled on my tiny tits and the other between my legs, eating me up like your favorite snack.

I hated how small my breasts were – rising just inches off my chest – but Kamsi, you rebuked me as you slid your tongue over my erect nipples, a purr humming from the depths of your throat as you took my entire breasts in your warm mouth.

You sucked and slurped on my breast like the Nile poured out from it, your eyes closed tight as you engulfed me in waves of pleasure.

Kamsi, you are a wizard your mouth. Your lips molded around my breast in a tight grip that made me shiver in slight tremors – the tingly feeling running down my spine and tucking itself in the warm bed of my pussy.

I tried to stay quiet, biting down on my lips to keep the screams at bay, but Bola, you didn't like that idea. You placed two stiff fingers on my clit and rubbed hard on it – and at the same time, thrust your tongue deep into my narrow passage that stretched and spread open at the jab of your stiff muscle. You shoved it in and out, my soul rising and dipping with it – the scream on my lips climbing to notes as thin as a needle.

Then you stopped thrusting and started wagging, sending your tongue left and right as you lashed inside of me. I've never had a tongue-lashing as bad as that. My pussy still ached even by morning – a small gift from you, I suppose, cause the pain left me floating throughout the day as I went on with my job – my pussy throbbing at the most unexpected moments, leaving me weak in the knees.

But you didn't stop there, Bola; you didn't let me off the hook that easily. You paused for seconds – seconds that seemed like eternities, then thrust back inside with a maddening rage that shook me to my core.

So, when I scream the name of the Lord in shrill notes and deep grunts, it doesn't come as a surprise. You did that, after all.

Today though, my mind wanders to one particular thing about you: your smile.

What was it about your smile that got me daydreaming? It was pretty, true, but that wasn't what held my gaze all night at the bar, nah. It wasn't just the pink hue of your lower lips against the dark top; it wasn't the soft way they trembled whenever our fingers touched, no, that wasn't it – it was the mystery that those lips of yours held that got me thinking about them, hours into the morning.

I'm sure I'm not the only one that had that thought. I think they all saw it, anyone that was fortunate to grace the pair as they glistened under the bright lights. They certainly left an impression on the viewer, that warm tingly, feeling that makes one believe they were the only person in the room – that they were the only ones that caught your eyes.

Cause that's how I felt when you looked at me and smiled.

It wasn't your everyday-typical smile. There was a way your lips lifted only on the right side, a slight glimpse of white teeth peeking. It left me confused and intrigued all at once. I saw that smile for the first at the bar, my eyes lingering on those luscious lips longer than they should; And later that night, while you had your hands on my thighs and your head deep in between my legs, I felt it on my lips – just before you dipped your nose in it, and took a deep breath of my scent.

You were the one that surprised me the most, Bola, cause you were as quiet as a mouse at the bar. Your eyes only met mine when they peeked through the rim of your glass, anytime you took a sip.

It was almost as if those dark eyes held a secret in them – like they knew something that could change the course of time; and then at the field, those secrets were spoken into the depths of my wet pussy as you moaned into it.

Maybe I shouldn't have followed you both to that field, resisted the urge when you asked me to take an 'innocent stroll' under the beautiful night sky… ran to my car. But at the bar, I was a ball of nerves ready to explode; every time your fingers grazed my bare thighs, or my arm or brushed against my breast – my whole body seemed to lose bits and parts of itself to you.

My panties were drenched by the time I was laying on the field, my heart racing like a thief when you, Bola, lifted my gown and pulled my panties down. Your eyes, so bright, sparkled like a kid seeing Santa for the first time when they glanced down at my pulsating sex.

Did you see my clit twitching? Did you see how wet you got me… how badly I wanted you?

I tried shutting my legs, my heart in my mouth as those dark eyes of yours ate me up. It shouldn't have mattered, I've fucked in public places more times than I can count, but there was something about the way your eyes peered into me; they stripped me down to my soul, and I was scared of what you would get to see.

Beautiful. Those words left your lips and I melted into the soil beneath me.

It wasn't just what you said that had me spellbound, it was also the way you touched me – your fingertips burning your feelings into my skin as they pulled my legs apart and dropped down to my center.

And then you Kamsi, maybe I shouldn't have lifted my arms as you pulled off my gown, the cold breeze dancing on my bare tits – its icy fingers wrapping around my nipples. Maybe

I should have stopped you as you stooped lower, but your lips crashed into mine, and my senses crashed right behind them.

It felt like I was breathing for the first time in my life, the hair on my skin standing on its end as I wrapped my arms around your neck.

How can a kiss feel so good? My pussy throbbed and twitched as your soft lips melted into mine, sucking on it with gentle pulls and hungry crushes.

***

If you enjoyed this snippet, click here to read the entire story.

The Place Between Her Legs

I glanced down at her breast. I didn't want to, but I couldn't help it; My eyes moved of their own free will, ignoring the nerve signals that ordered them to look up – to focus on her face, her freckled nose, and those brilliant blue eyes.

But they didn't listen.

They traveled down to her chest, taking in the soft curves of her tits as they strained against her cotton singlet; and then on her large, erect nipples that peeked through the thin material.

My heart was racing, banging against the bony cages of my ribs in fast beats – fast beats that left me breathless and my hands clammy with sweat.

"What time is your flight?" Hanna stretched forward, leaning over as she picked up one of my shirts at the far end of the bed – her chest almost kissing the sheets.

"12 pm," I whispered. That was all I could do to stop myself from choking as her bare breasts came into full view.

She had really pale skin, but her breasts were two shades lighter, and her nipples were the brightest of pinks. Those hard buds swung in soft motions, back and forth, moving with the sway of her breasts as she leaned forward some more before sitting right up.

Did she want me to see them, to see that she was hard for me – that she wanted me?

"This sucks." Hanna bit down on her lower lips, her brows curved inwards at its head, wrinkling her forehead, "I wish you could stay a little longer."

My gaze lingered on those lips and then thoughts – weird thoughts – started forming in the deepest part of my mind, painting vivid images with vibrant colors and deep strokes.

I wasn't meant to be having such thoughts. I'd fought them off many times already, denying their soft whispers as they called me that name: queer.

For years I'd won the battle, shut them off, screamed in denial till their whispers were nothing but a faint buzz, but Hanna was the exception.

I'm weak around her, always have been; My walls crumble around her feet, one brick at a time, tumbling down to reveal the truth – the one truth that I had hidden ever since I was a kid – ever since I felt it, that rush that raced through me like a bullet train, that coursed through me when I had my first crush on Grace.

I was told it wasn't "normal". Mom called me confused when I told her how I felt about Grace – how I wanted to marry her when I grew up. At first, she laughed it off, but when I introduced Dora as my girlfriend a few years later, she dragged me to church for deliverance.

But Hanna... she was the exception. Everything about her made it feel okay; made me feel okay.

"I wish I could too," I picked up one of my shirts and folded it into a tiny square, my eyes drifting away from hers, "But my student visa expired, so that's that."

She exhaled in a loud sigh, throwing her head back and exposing her slender neck to me.

Was she doing it on purpose, tempting me with the parts of her that I wanted the most – that I had fantasized about – that I was hungry for?

I wanted to touch her, to wrap my long fingers around her throat and press my lips against it till she shivered all over.

"Will you ever come back to the states?" She leaned forward and looked straight at me.

"Maybe…" I shoved the cloth into my suitcase, "but it might be a little difficult."

Then Hanna stood up abruptly, a bunch of my clothes scattering all over the floor.

"We can't spend your last night folding clothes," she walked over to my side of the bed and grabbed me by my hands, pulling me up to my feet "What do you want to do? Anything! Let's make your last night memorable."

I couldn't speak. The words were there, they had formed deep inside me, crawled their way up my throat, and climbed right up to the tip of my tongue, but I couldn't say them.

"Kamara?" She squeezed my hands in her, her heat sipping into me. It raced from my fingertips – up to my arms – and then down the length of my spine.

Those thoughts – those crazy thoughts – ran to every corner of my mind, filling up every space with crystal clear images of Hanna's lean body underneath mine as I kiss her, taste her, eat her – till there was nothing left but images of her.

"Anything?"

"Anything."

I swallowed hard, my breathing turning rasp and shallow, my hands shaking in hers as I leaned forward and covered her lips with mine.

The world burst into flames of colors, and my heart along with it – flowing with emotions that seemed to have no names but felt so familiar, like it had always been there with me – lying dormant, underneath all the pile of denials and self-hate – but there regardless.

If you enjoyed this snippet, click here to read the entire story.

About Author

Jasmine Emelie is a Nigerian Amateur erotica writer. She is based in the beautiful city of Ibadan and spends most of her day, lounging around, watching movies and reading books.

Pls, make me scream is her third short story and will be a part an upcoming Erotica anthology *"We should all be fucking".* Look forward to it.

And if you enjoyed this short read, then kindly leave a review or rate this book. That little act of kindness will help this book in more ways than you can imagine. Thank you.

Printed in Great Britain
by Amazon

84853596R00031